The Cookie Tree

By Jay Williams · Illustrated by Blake Hampton

PARENTS' MAGAZINE PRESS · NEW YORK

𝕿HE VILLAGE of Owlgate was quiet and tidy, and nothing surprising ever happened there. Everything had a place, and everything was in its place. Everybody knew why things happened and everything happened just as it was sup-

posed to. Nothing surprising ever happened because nothing surprising was allowed to happen.

"That way," said the people of Owlgate, with satisfaction, "you always know where you are."

ONE MORNING, in the center of the village, a strange tree appeared. It had not been there the night before, but it was there this morning. It was a small tree with bark that shone like silver, and round golden leaves that twinkled in the sun. And under every leaf there hung what looked like a chocolate cookie.

A girl named Meg was the first to see it. Her window, tucked under the heavy thatch of her house, faced the square, and when she peeped out of the window early in the morning, there stood the tree.

Meg got dressed quickly and ran down to the square. She walked round and round the tree, and then she went to find her mother.

"MOTHER," she said, "is it all right if I pick a cookie?"

Her mother was bustling about in the kitchen, frying eggs and toasting bread. "You mean pick *out* a cookie, dear," she said. "And not before breakfast."

"No, I mean *pick* one. There is a cookie tree in the village square."

Her father had just sat down to the breakfast table. He began to laugh. "What a good imagination my little girl has!"

"Well, come and see," said Meg.

WHEN her father and mother saw the tree, they blinked.

"It wasn't here last night," said her mother. "Where on earth did it come from?"

"Maybe a magician sent it," said Meg. "Maybe it's a present to the village."

But her parents weren't listening. "Why should a tree bear cookies?" said her father, in a worried voice. "What can it be for?"

"I don't know," said Meg, "but can I eat one?"

"Certainly not!" said her father. "They may be poisonous. I'll go and call the Mayor."

The Mayor was a brisk and lively little man, and he was briskly and livelily trimming his beard. He looked in the mirror with his head on one side and snipped away, and suddenly he saw Meg's father looking over his shoulder. He gave a jump and cut off too much beard on that side.

"Now see what you've made me do," he said, crossly. "I hope you've got a good reason for startling me at this hour. Or any other hour," he added.

"You won't believe me," said Meg's father, "but there's a tree covered with cookies in the village square."

WHO left it there?" cried the Mayor.
"I don't know," said Meg's father. "But you'd
better have a look at it."

The Mayor put on his red gown and his golden
chain and hurried out. By the time he got to the

square, quite a lot of people had gathered. Some of them pointed and some of them laughed. Many looked worried and whispered together.

MORGAN THE MILLER had come from his mill, dusting flour off his thick arms. "It's a joke," he shouted, roaring with amusement.

" 'Tisn't natural," groaned Basil the Butcher. "Ghostly, that's what it is."

"A warning of trouble to come," said old Mrs. Gape the Grocer, shaking her head.

CHILDREN had squeezed between the grownups. They stood beside Meg, peering and giggling, looking with delight at the silver tree with its golden leaves.

Meg's friend, Janet, said, "What's happened? Did somebody plant a cookie?"

"Is it yours?" a big boy named Conn said to Meg. "I'll trade you my knife with the bone handle for it."

"Can we climb it?" asked a little boy named Dylan.

"I think a magician sent it," Meg answered. "I think it's a present to the village."

All the children nodded to each other. That explained everything.

THE MAYOR pushed his way through the crowd. He stared up at the tree, mopping his face with a silk handkerchief.

"A cookie tree?" he exclaimed. "Impossible!"

"Why?" asked Meg, boldly.

"I have never seen one before," said the Mayor, tugging at his lopsided beard. "You have never seen one before. Nobody has ever seen one before, and there is no mention of one anywhere in the Town Records. We must get to the bottom of this. Who put it here? Why? What is it for?"

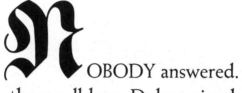

OBODY answered.

Then the small boy, Dylan, piped, "It's a present from a magician."

"Nonsense!" shouted the Mayor. "Why would a magician send a cookie tree here? What is it *for?* Everything must be for something. But this makes no sense at all."

"Send for the Village Councillors," suggested Basil the Butcher.

MEN ran off to find them.

In a wide street of tall houses lived Finn the Fat. When he was called, he slowly and deliberately finished eating a large steak, wiped his lips, brushed his hair, put on his long, wide cloak and slowly came.

In a narrow dark street lived Thelwin the Thin. He was as thin as paper. He ate almost nothing, and when the messenger came for him he was breakfasting on the smell of bacon and a glass of water.

Alwyn the Ancient was so old that he looked like a wrinkle with a man around the edges of it. He lived in an old, old house, and two messengers had to help him get up from his chair. But he walked very spryly once he was up, and got to the square as soon as the others did.

The three Councillors examined the tree from one side and then from the other. They stroked their chins thoughtfully. The Mayor rapped his staff on the cobblestones.

WELL, sirs," he said, "what would you say we have here?"

"Hm, hm," began Thelwin the Thin. "It seems to be a tree covered with sweet biscuits or small cakes of a dark brown and glossy color."

"They appear to be growing on the tree," pointed out Finn the Fat.

Alwyn the Ancient stood on tiptoe. Carefully he broke off the lowest of the cookies. Everybody went, "Ooooh."

He popped it into his mouth and chewed. Everybody chewed with him. He swallowed. Everybody swallowed.

"Without making any rash statements," he quavered, "I would say that that was a chocolate cookie."

Everybody went, "Aaaah."

"I have never seen anything like it," said Thelwin the Thin, doubtfully.

"I don't believe in it," snapped Finn the Fat.

"It should not exist—but it does," said Alwyn the Ancient.

The Mayor hopped on one foot, as he always did when he was excited.

ENTLEMEN!" he said. "What we must know is, what is it FOR? Everything has to be for something. Everything has its reason, and until we know the reason for this we cannot live happily and peacefully in Owlgate. The reason for the well is to give us water. The reason for the sun is to grow our crops. The reason—"

"The reason for a Mayor is to make speeches," put in Alwyn the Ancient.

The Mayor hopped on both feet as he always did when he couldn't think of anything more to say.

"This tree," said Thelwin, "could be a prognostication of some perpending disaster."

"Just what I was going to say," nodded Finn.

"In other words," said Alwyn, "a warning of trouble to come."

"Aha! What did I tell you?" muttered Mrs. Gape the Grocer.

The Mayor turned pale. "Then what we want is deeds, not words. We must send for Sir Owen the Lord of Owlgate."

$\mathfrak{S}$IR OWEN lived in a strong gray castle on a rocky hill above the village. Someone ran to fetch him, and soon he came striding down the cobbled street, his bright sword hanging by his side. He frowned at the tree.

"What's all this, hey?" he barked. "Witchcraft!"

At the word, everybody moved quickly back. Everybody except the children who were busy looking at the tree. Its leaves fluttered and twinkled in the sun, and all the chocolate cookies rustled with a crisp, delicious sound.

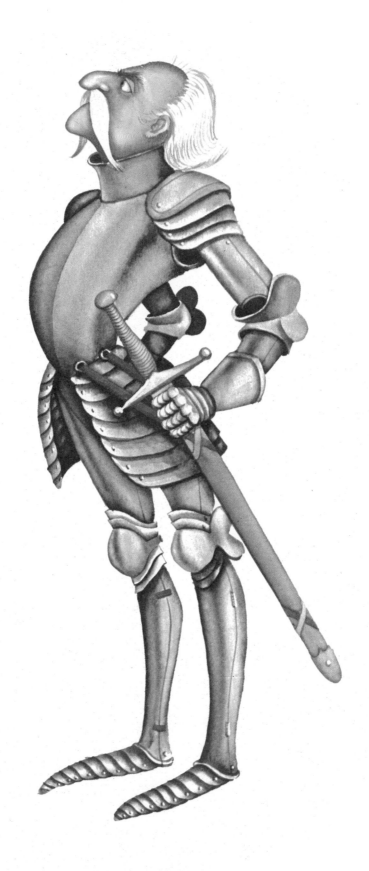

THIS has always been a quiet village," said Sir Owen. "And that's how we want to keep it, hey? We want no goblin trees, no demonizing and devilry in Owlgate. Cut it down!"

"Yes, yes," crooned Mrs. Gape the Grocer. "Down with it and to the fire with it."

"One moment, my lord," said Alwyn the Ancient. "If this is a warning, a sign that something strange is about to happen, then perhaps we should wait to find out what it is."

"No strangeness and changeness here!" cried Basil the Butcher. "Let things stay as they are. Don't touch the tree, or something worse may come."

"On the other hand," put in Thelwin, "since it is rather pretty, and certainly very unusual, perhaps we should send it to the king."

"Ah, there's a thought," laughed Morgan the Miller. He clapped his hands so that a cloud of flour rose up and made everybody sneeze. "The king will give us gold and silver for it. Owlgate will be his favorite village."

Ａ S for me," growled Finn the Fat,
turning his back on the tree, "I don't believe in it,
and therefore I will not discuss it."

On every side, people began to argue. Some said
one thing and some another. Thelwyn, Alwyn, the
Mayor and Sir Owen put their heads together and
began talking excitedly.

THE children moved closer to the tree, until they were all around it in a ring. Meg put out a finger and stroked the silvery bark. The smallest children stood on tiptoe to watch. The bigger ones looked at each other out of the corners of their eyes.

Meg took hold of the smooth trunk and gave it a little shake. The leaves whispered and the chocolate cookies rattled.

The boy, Conn, put his hands on the trunk and gave it a big shake. Other boys and girls stretched out their arms and helped him.

Down fell cookies, pattering softly on the cobblestones with a noise like many bare feet.

𝔑ONE of the townspeople noticed, for they were deep in argument. At last, the Mayor waved his hands in the air and shouted, "Silence, good citizens. Silence!"

Everyone became quiet.

"My friends," said the Mayor, "we have come to a decision. In fact, since three of anything is better than one, we have come to three decisions. Everything should have a purpose. We now have three purposes for this tree. Knowing the purposes, we know how to act. Since we fear that the tree may be magical, we shall cut it down so that it can do us no harm."

MRS. GAPE led her friends in applause.

"However, since it may be a warning, we shall keep it in the Town Hall for three days and watch it."

Basil the Butcher and a number of other people clapped their hands in agreement.

"And after that, we shall send it to the king," finished the Mayor.

Morgan the Miller and his friends cheered between floury sneezes.

"Very well, Sir Owen," said the Mayor. "Please begin by cutting down the tree."

SIR OWEN drew his sharp sword. He stepped forward. His eyes became round with astonishment.

"What tree?" he said.

There was no sign of it. The cobblestones were bare and smooth. Only a few crumbs rolled in the breeze.

"What has become of it?" gasped the Mayor.

ROWS and rows of widely grinning children looked at him without saying anything.

"Where has it gone, hey? Speak up!" bellowed Sir Owen.

"Please, sir, it just quietly folded up smaller and smaller and then disappeared," said Meg.

"After we ate the cookies," added her friend, Janet.

"But—but what was it for? Everything must be for something," stammered the Mayor.

The little boy, Conn, stuck out his tongue and licked chocolate off his lips.

"*That* was what it was for," he said.

Somewhere, a magician smiled with satisfaction.